PUFFIN BOOKS

DANCING SHOES
MODEL DANCERS

Antonia Barber was born in London and grew up in Sussex. While studying English at London University, she spent her evenings at the Royal Opera House, where her father worked, watching the ballet and meeting many famous dancers. She married a fellow student and lived in New York before settling back in England. She has three children, including a daughter who did ballet from the age of three and attended the Royal Ballet School Junior Classes at Sadler's Wells.

Her best-known books are *The Ghosts*, which was runner-up for the Carnegie Medal and was filmed as *The Amazing Mr Blunden*, and *The Mousehole Cat*. She has also written *Tales from the Ballet*.

Antonia lives in an old oast house in Kent and a little fisherman's cottage in Cornwall.

If you like dancing and making friends, you'll love

DANCING SHOES

Lucy Lambert – Lou to her friends – dreams of one day becoming a great ballerina. Find out if Lucy's dream comes true in:

DANCING SHOES: LESSONS FOR LUCY

DANCING SHOES: INTO THE SPOTLIGHT

DANCING SHOES: FRIENDS AND RIVALS

DANCING SHOES: OUT OF STEP

DANCING SHOES: MAKING THE GRADE

DANCING SHOES: LUCY'S NEXT STEP

DANCING SHOES: BEST FOOT FORWARD

DANCING SHOES: TIME TO DANCE

DANCING SHOES: IN A SPIN

And look out for more DANCING SHOES titles
coming soon

Antonia Barber

Dancing Shoes
Model Dancers

Illustrated by Biz Hull

PUFFIN BOOKS

PUFFIN BOOKS

Published by the Penguin Group
Penguin Books Ltd, 27 Wrights Lane, London W8 5TZ, England
Penguin Putnam Inc., 375 Hudson Street, New York, New York 10014, USA
Penguin Books Australia Ltd, Ringwood, Victoria, Australia
Penguin Books Canada Ltd, 10 Alcorn Avenue, Toronto, Ontario, Canada M4V 3B2
Penguin Books (NZ) Ltd, Private Bag 102902, NSMC, Auckland, New Zealand

On the World Wide Web at www.penguin.com

Penguin Books Ltd, Registered Offices: Harmondsworth, Middlesex, England

First published 2000
1 3 5 7 9 10 8 6 4 2

Typeset in 15/22 Monotype Calisto

Made and printed in England by Clays Ltd, St Ives plc

British Library Cataloguing in Publication Data
A CIP catalogue record for this book is available from the British Library

ISBN 0–141–30530–4

Chapter One

'It must be brilliant having your own mobile phone!' said Lou.

Emma nodded. 'You could talk to your friends any time,' she agreed, 'wherever you were . . . and wherever they were . . .'

'Only if they had one too.'

'If they didn't, you could call their ordinary phone,' said Emma. 'Like Shell did just now.'

'She was lucky we were home already, and that you were having tea with us.'

'She was phoning from her car,' said Emma. 'Her mum was still driving her home . . .' She thought about it, then went on, 'Wouldn't it be *great* to have a mobile at school?'

Lou laughed. 'I don't think Jumbo

Jones would stand for a lot of phones going beep in class.'

'I suppose not.'

'It's different for Shell,' Lou said, 'doing all that modelling and stuff. She says she needs a mobile so her mum and dad know when to pick her up.'

Lou and Emma had met Shell Pink (whose real name was Michelle Pinkham) at a Summer Dance School and they had become firm friends. But her life was very different from theirs.

Lucy Lambert and Emma Browne lived in the same big London house. Emma lived upstairs with her parents and her older brother, who went away to school. Lou lived with her mum, Jenny, and her little brother, Charlie, in the basement flat. Both girls loved dancing and Lou had set her heart on becoming a famous ballerina. But they had only one ballet class each week at the Maple School of Ballet nearby, while Shell's whole life seemed to revolve around dancing. Her mother had once run her own troupe of dancers and since retiring she had put all her efforts into making her daughter a musical star. Shell went to ballet, tap and modern dance classes. She had piano lessons and singing lessons. She performed at festivals and won lots of prizes. In her spare time, she even modelled clothes for magazines.

Emma said it made her feel tired just *thinking* about Shell's busy life. But the little blonde girl seemed to take it all in her stride.

'Jem's got the right word for Shell,' said Lou. 'He says she's dynamic.'

Lou always felt a little anxious about

the way he admired Shell. Jem Sinclair was her other best friend, after Emma, and he was the only boy in their ballet class. Lou wanted him to be her dance partner when they grew up. But Jem said he was only doing ballet to help him get into stage school. He said he wanted to dance in musicals – like Shell – and Lou worried that if he did, she would end up without a partner. Then she would have to be a cygnet or a sylphide instead of being a prima ballerina. She could imagine herself doing arabesques in a white embroidered tutu . . . and falling over because she had no partner to help her balance. Of course, there *was* Paul, she thought, but he was really Emma's friend.

'Why didn't you tell Shell about Paul?' she asked. 'I reckon if she knew you were best friends, she would have invited him too.'

Emma went a bit pink. 'We're not *best* friends,' she said. '*You're* my best friend. Paul is . . . well, he's just a friend, like Jem is.'

Lou raised her eyebrows.

'Stop teasing me!' said Emma. 'You promised you wouldn't!'

Paul Purvis was a new friend. He was two years older than Lou and Emma and went to a different school. But he did go to their ballet school and he was a really good dancer. He had just won a place at the Royal Ballet Junior School, which made him seem very special.

'I'm sure Shell would want to meet him,' said Lou, 'and I bet Paul would like to see *West Side Story*.'

'I don't think he's very interested in

6

musicals,' said Emma. 'I think he only really likes ballet. And in any case,' she added, 'if I tell Shell about him, she'll invite him just to see what he's like . . . and then she might tease me and it will spoil everything!'

Lou sighed. She knew how much her friend hated to be teased, or even to be the centre of attention.

'Oh, all right!' she said. 'I won't tell Shell, and I'll warn Jem not to either.'

She didn't want anything to spoil what was going to be a fabulous weekend. Because Shell's phone call had been to invite her three friends to see *West Side Story*, their favourite musical, live on stage next Saturday afternoon. And as if that wasn't enough, they were all going back to Shell's house after the show to have a barbecue in the garden and to stay overnight.

Chapter Two

'I hope it's the Cadillac,' said Jem. 'I've always wanted to ride in that. People will stare as we go by and I shall wave like royalty.'

They were watching from Emma's front window, squinting along the street to catch the first glimpse of the Pinkhams' car.

Shell's dad had made a fortune selling American cars to pop stars. He had brought his daughter to the Summer

School in a huge pink Cadillac covered in gleaming chrome. Jem was mad about cars and Lou thought he seemed even more thrilled about riding in Mr Pinkham's car than he was about going to see *West Side Story*.

They had all got ready in a rush because Shell's mum had phoned late the evening before to say there was a change of plan and could they be ready by ten o'clock instead of two? She said she would explain everything when she arrived.

They were so busy watching for the pink Cadillac that they didn't notice the smart people-carrier until it pulled up outside the house. A small head with a mass of blue frizzy hair popped out of the back window and a hand waved wildly.

They all stared.

'Its Shell!' said Lou.

'So it is.' Emma could hardly believe the vision before them.

'Wow,' said Jem. 'What *has* she done to her hair?'

'Do you think she wears it like that for school?' asked Lou as they stampeded out on to the front steps.

Shell bounced out of the big car and raced up to meet them. Close to, they saw that the blue hair was threaded through with plaited ribbons of blue, green and silver. The effect was astonishing.

'What about the hair then?' she demanded when she had finished hugging them. 'Fantastic or what?' And she laughed her shrill laugh.

'Amazing!' said Lou.

'Mind-boggling!' said Jem, and Emma

asked nervously, 'Do you wear it like that for school?'

Shell laughed again even louder. 'They'd kill me if I did!' she told them. 'My school's dead proper . . . It's just for today's shoot!'

'But the colour,' said Emma.

'Some sort of veggie dye,' said Shell. 'It'll wash out before I'm due back. Meantime, pretty cool, eh?'

They had to admit that it was.

Lou was just about to ask Shell what she meant by 'the shoot', when Mrs Pinkham came up behind her daughter. She wore tight trousers with very high-heeled shoes and had a mass of red hair like a big dandelion puff. She always made Lou think of an exotic bird she had once seen at the zoo. But she greeted them warmly, hugging and kissing them as she teetered on the steps.

Lou and Emma's mothers had come out to meet them and were gazing rather nervously at Shell's hair.

Mrs Pinkham flashed them both a brilliant smile. 'Sorry to rush off,' she said, 'but we've got a photo shoot for a dance-wear catalogue at half-past. It should have been done yesterday but the photographer crumped his motorbike on the way to the studio and ended up in casualty!' She laughed as if it was all a great joke.

'I hope he isn't badly hurt,' said Mrs Browne.

'Hopping about like Long John Silver,' said Shell's mum, 'but still in one piece!' She laughed again. 'But I've got it sorted,' she went on. 'Your kids can watch while we do the shoot, I've swapped our matinée tickets for tonight's show and we'll have the barbecue for tomorrow's lunch. So, no problem. Except that we *must* rush, because the traffic is something awful.'

They grabbed their bags from the hallway. Lou and Emma gave their mums a quick kiss goodbye and two minutes later they were all waving from the back window of the people-carrier.

'Sorry about the shoot,' said Shell as they threaded their way through the London traffic. 'It'll be really boring for you.'

'Sounds great,' said Jem. 'I've never seen a photo shoot.'

Lou and Emma said they hadn't either.

'Oh, well,' said Shell, 'it might be fun the first time, but when you do it a lot it's just hard work.'

The car was being driven by Shell's dad, a short, stocky man in a flowery shirt. He drove fast and seemed to know his way around the backstreets. Before long they were pulling up outside a big warehouse building down by the river.

'I'll pick you up after the show tonight, Jackie,' he called cheerfully as they clambered out.

Shell's mum gave him a wave. 'Righto,

Shane,' she said. 'We'll get a cab to the theatre.'

The big car roared away, nearly colliding with a taxi that suddenly appeared round the corner. The taxi swerved and they heard a crash from inside as it came to a halt.

Shell's mum flung open the taxi door, crying, 'Is that you, Barry?'

There was a man lying on the taxi floor under a pile of camera cases. He glowered at Mrs Pinkham. 'Was that your Shane, Jackie?' he said. 'Driving like a maniac as usual! Wouldn't be surprised if he's broken me other leg.'

Shell's mum clucked and made sympathetic noises as she helped the man out of the taxi. He handed her a crutch and they saw that he had one foot in plaster. As he struggled to balance himself, it was clear that he wouldn't be able to manage the camera cases, so Jem went to lift them out. The girls helped to carry them, while Mrs Pinkham paid off the taxi.

'Thanks, Jackie,' said the photographer. 'I owe you one.'

'Don't worry,' said Shell's mum. 'I'll

charge it up to my Shane . . . Teach him not to go tearing round the way he does.' She pressed a bell beside a door in the wall and a mumbled voice answered.

'It's Jackie and Shell . . . Oh, and Barry's with us!' she shouted into the intercom.

A buzzer buzzed and Shell's mum pushed the door open.

Chapter Three

The warehouse had a rather creaky lift.
Lou thought this was just as well, because
otherwise it would have taken half the
morning just to get the photographer up
the stairs.

The studio was a high-ceilinged room
on the top floor, with big windows facing
out over the docks. There were lots of
lights overhead and a small gallery at one
end. In the centre of the room stood
three girls with hairstyles just like Shell's,

only one was pink, one was mauve and one was a rather startling shade of green. They were already dressed in modern dance gear to match their hair. They hardly glanced at the newcomers, but Lou, Emma and Jem couldn't help staring at them as Mrs Pinkham found them seats in the little gallery out of the way.

A young woman came in carrying a clipboard. 'Get a move on, Shell,' she said. 'You're keeping us all waiting!'

Shell waved one hand carelessly. 'Barry won't be ready for ages,' she said, and disappeared through a door at one end of the studio, just as a boy with his hair spiked like a hedgehog came the other way.

Barry was struggling to fix the tripods for his cameras and Shell's mum went to help him. The main door flew open again and in swept an older woman talking loudly into a mobile phone. They heard her say, 'Well, try again! We need them here by lunchtime. We're already running a day late!' She snapped her mobile phone shut and said to the other woman, 'You were supposed to get it sorted last night!'

The younger woman was busily tweaking the ribbons in the hair of the mauve girl. She looked annoyed. 'I left messages on their answer machines,' she said. 'I sent faxes. I've e-mailed them . . . Maybe they've all gone away for the weekend.'

'So what do we do for the ballet section?'

'Can't we use the same models?'

The older woman gave her a withering look. 'With those hairstyles?' she said.

'Don't be ridiculous!' and she swept out again, tapping a new number into the mobile as she went.

'This is as good as being at the theatre,' muttered Jem.

'It's brilliant,' said Lou, 'and Shell gets to do this sort of thing all the time.' As she spoke, Shell reappeared, dressed in a snazzy blue and green leotard.

There were huge sheets of coloured paper taped to the walls and spilling out across the floor. Against these backgrounds, the young woman began to arrange the models in different poses. She made them all leap in the air with their arms and legs thrown wide. They practised it a few times and then she told them to 'take five'.

'I didn't know they really said that,' said Jem.

'I didn't know models had to jump about,' said Emma. 'I thought they just stood around.'

The photographer seemed to be having problems. Balancing on the crutch, it took him ages to change a lens. He kept muttering under his breath. Suddenly he looked around. 'Where are those other kids?' he demanded. It took Lou, Emma and Jem a few moments to realize that he meant them.

'We're up here,' called Lou from the little gallery.

'Then get down here sharpish, love,' he said. 'I could do with some help.'

They raced down the narrow steps, almost tripping over one another in their hurry. Barry gave Jem a case of lenses, Emma got the filters and Lou was put in charge of 'odds and ends'.

'Keep back out of the way until I need something,' he told them. 'Then jump to it and bring them where I can reach them. That way I won't spend half the morning hobbling about trying to reach my gear.'

The make-up girl finished giving the models a last fluff-over with the powder puff and then the fun began.

The models posed, they jumped, they did cartwheels, they turned somersaults. All the time Barry clicked away with his cameras, calling out instructions. 'Head up, the green one . . . lovely, lovely . . . A really big smile now . . . Go on, dazzle me with those shiny teeth . . . That's better . . . Now, once more, as high as you can get . . .' And every now and then he would call for lenses or filters, and Jem and Emma would bring the cases.

Lou found herself holding a big silver
reflector which Barry said would 'fill in'
the light so that there wasn't too much
contrast. Lou didn't quite understand this,
but it was great fun to be helping instead
of just watching from the gallery.

After each set of shots, the models would disappear into the dressing room. The background colour would be changed, new film would be loaded into the cameras and then the models would return in a different set of leotards. Sometimes, instead of leaping about, they played with coloured hoops or balls – anything that would make the pictures in the dance catalogue look bright and exciting. It was very tiring work, even for Lou, Emma and Jem.

They began to get quite hungry, and Shell's mum said they would break for lunch after the next shot. She phoned for some burgers and sandwiches and drinks. Then, just as she was finishing her phone call, the main door swung open and the older woman swept in again. She took one look at Lou, Emma and Jem and stopped dead with her mouth open. Then she turned quite white.

'Why didn't anyone bother to *tell* me that *they* were *here*?' she shouted.

'Calm down, Elinor,' said Mrs Pinkham. 'You've got it all wrong –'

'*I've* got it wrong!' yelled the woman. '*I* have spent the *whole* morning phoning around, trying to find a *single* child model who hasn't gone away for the Bank Holiday weekend, and *all the time* they were in here and no one had even *bothered* to tell me that they had *arrived*!'

Shell's mum let her rage on until she finally ran out of steam. Then she said very calmly, 'Elinor, you're not listening. The kids are just friends of Shell's. I brought them along because we're going on to see a show after the shoot. They're *not* your models.'

The woman stared at her in disbelief.
Then she frowned and took a long hard
look at Lou, Emma and Jem, who stood
there feeling really uncomfortable. At last
she turned back to Shell's mum and
smiled a grim smile. 'Well, they are now,'
she said.

Chapter Four

Lou, Emma and Jem sat with Shell and
Barry on the little terrace outside the
studio. The other models had gone home.

There was a table with chairs and a
shady umbrella. The food and drinks had
arrived and they were all busy munching
and admiring the view over the sparkling
waters of the river. Mrs Pinkham and
Elinor had stayed behind in the studio
and Lou could hear some sort of
argument going on.

After a while, Shell's mum came out to join them. She sat down and said, 'I'm sorry Elinor got so steamed up just now. I hope she didn't scare you.'

'I thought she was going to throw us out,' said Emma.

'I've told them she's always like that,'

said Shell, wiping tomato sauce off her
chin. 'She flies off the handle over the
least thing. Nobody takes any notice.'

Shell's mum gave one of her loud
laughs, which sounded just like Shell's.
'Well, she certainly doesn't want to throw
you out,' she told Emma. 'The thing is,
she badly needs your help. You see, this
shoot would've happened yesterday if
that idiot hadn't come off his bike.' She
smiled at Barry, who scowled back. 'With
him in casualty all afternoon getting his
foot plastered,' she went on, 'we had to
put the shoot off until today. But the
models doing the ballet gear couldn't
come. They were all competing in some
dance festival up north. Elinor has been
phoning around ever since, trying to find
some other kids, but everyone seems to
be away . . .'

31

'Did Elinor think *we* were the models?' asked Lou. She thought it was rather flattering to be mistaken for a model.

'Well, it's not just that,' said Shell's mum. 'Elinor wants you lot to do the modelling for her. She says you're the right shape and you've got the right sort of faces and hair and all.' She paused and waited to see how they would take the idea.

'You mean,' said Lou, 'that Emma and Jem and me . . . we actually get to model the ballet gear . . . for the dance catalogue?'

'We wouldn't know how,' said Emma, frowning. 'I mean, all that leaping about and doing somersaults . . .'

'Oh, it won't be like that,' said Shell. 'That zany stuff is just for modern dance gear. The ballet is all *pliés* and *tendus*. You know, standing around looking cool and elegant in frilly tutus.'

'Unbelievable!' said Lou, wide-eyed with excitement. 'Oh, *please* can we do it?'

'If you want to,' said Mrs Pinkham, 'but we'll have to ask your mums first.'

'Well, I'm game,' said Jem. 'My gran won't mind, but I'm not standing around in a frilly tutu!'

Lou gave him a look.

Shell's mum got out her mobile and called each of their numbers in turn. There was no reply from Lou's mum, which threw Lou into an agony of suspense in case she wasn't allowed to do it. But luckily, when they called Emma's number, they found that Jenny Lambert and Charlie had just popped upstairs to have a quiet lunch with Mrs Browne.

The mothers talked for a while and then Mrs Pinkham handed the phone to Lou. 'Your mum wants a word.'

Lou grabbed the phone. 'Mum?'

'Do you and Emma really want to do this modelling?'

'Oh yes. Please, *please*, Mum!'

'OK, OK! So long as you are happy about it.'

Mrs Browne spoke to Emma, who was still a bit nervous, but said she did want to do it if Lou and Jem were going to.

She gave the phone back to Shell's mum and they heard her say, 'Shall I act for you? I'll get them the very best terms.'

The mothers seemed to agree and a moment later Mrs Pinkham was talking to Jem's gran.

'You'll be all right if my mum is acting for you,' Shell told them. 'Elinor's desperate. She'll pay whatever Mum asks.'

Lou was a bit puzzled about the acting. No one had mentioned any acting . . .

Emma also seemed confused. 'Who has to pay?' she asked. 'I didn't know anyone had to pay.'

'Well, it's not *you*,' said Shell, 'so don't look so worried.' When Emma didn't stop frowning, she explained, '*You're* the ones who get paid. The people doing the dance-gear catalogue pay *you* to do the modelling. Did you think models worked for nothing?'

'But we're not models,' said Emma.

Shell laughed. She seemed to be finding it really funny. 'But you are now, Em,' she said.

'Wait a minute,' said Lou slowly. 'Let's get this straight. Are you saying that we get to put on a load of fabulous ballet stuff – fancy tutus and all that – we get to have our pictures taken and be in a catalogue, and on top of all that we get *paid*?'

'Too right you do!' said Shell.

'Oh, *unbelievable*,' said Lou, flopping

back in her chair and gazing up at the blue sky overhead. She sighed. 'I know I must be dreaming this,' she said. 'I just hope I don't wake up until it's all over!'

Chapter Five

Lou stared at herself in the mirror. Her hair had been brushed until it shone like silk and plaited into a crown on top of her head. The hairdresser sprayed it lightly to keep every hair in place and fixed a little tiara on top.

'There,' she said. 'You look beautiful.'

Well, I certainly don't look much like me, thought Lou. The face looking back at her wore make-up and pink lipstick; the eyelashes were long and dark with mascara.

'I look awfully grown up,' she said doubtfully.

The hairdresser smiled. 'Don't worry,' she said. 'You need make-up because of the bright lights. Without it you'd look all pale and washed out. It's like being on the stage.'

Emma took her place in the chair and watched in some alarm as her pale skin became decidedly rosy.

Then it was Jem's turn. Lou thought he might make a fuss about having make-up put on, but he just shrugged.

'Where's the problem?' he said. 'I mean, if you want to go on the stage you're going to spend half your life either putting make-up on or taking it off. It goes with the job.'

It seemed that they were going to model the most glamorous tutus first.

'Those are the pictures for the big full-page spreads,' Shell told them, while her mum helped them to dress. 'They do them first while you're still bright-eyed.'

Emma and Lou were wearing identical white tutus, and both wore the little tiaras. Out in the studio they found a huge background photo of a misty lake taped to the wall, and they had to pose in ballet positions with their eyes cast down like the swans in *Swan Lake*.

Lou was so excited, she found it hard to look serious.

'Stop smiling,' said Barry, clicking away with his camera. 'You're a mysterious swan, love, not a cheery chicken!'

This remark sent both Lou and Emma off into fits of giggles that they couldn't stop. They had to 'take five' while they

calmed down and got dabbed with
powder all over again.

'Cut out the sarcasm, Barry,' said Mrs
Pinkham, who, with Shell's help, had
taken charge of the camera lenses and

things. 'These kids aren't professionals and they're not used to wise-cracking photographers.'

'Sorry!' said Lou. She felt she wasn't making a very good job of being a model.

'Not your fault, love,' said Shell's mum. 'Long John Silver here should know better than to set you off laughing.'

The two girls took up their pose again and Lou tried her best to look mysterious.

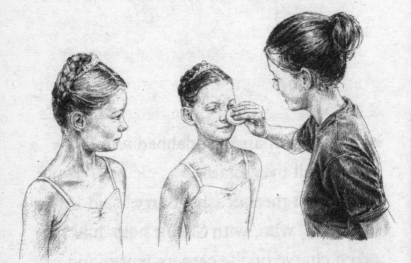

Modelling really was much harder than it looked, she thought, even when you didn't have to stand on your hands or turn somersaults.

After the first few shots, Jem came to join them wearing dark tights and a loose white top. Barry seemed to be taking dozens of pictures, far more than he could possibly need for the catalogue. Lou wondered if he would let them have some of the spare ones, but she didn't like to ask.

Soon they were back in the dressing room, changing into new tutus. This time Lou's had a bodice decorated with bands of ribbon and tiny rosebuds on the tulle of the skirt. Emma's was pale mauve and had little sprays of lilac flowers.

Lou sighed. 'Do you think we could tell them we don't want to be paid,' she said, 'we'd just like to keep the tutus instead?'

'I expect they'd be much too expensive,' said Emma wistfully. She really loved the lilac flowers.

Lou could have stood in front of the big mirror for hours, admiring herself in the rosebud tutu and dreaming of the day when she would wear one just like it on a real stage, in front of a wildly cheering audience. But they had to hurry back into the studio to pose by another big fuzzy photograph: this time it seemed to be some sort of snow palace. Barry clicked away and called out instructions all the time.

'Head up a bit, Rosebud . . . Bit more to the left, Lilac Fairy . . . Give us the other lens, Jackie . . . OK now, heads up . . . Look a bit snooty . . . Great! Great!

Now let's have a smile . . . Brilliant! OK, that'll do for that lot.'

And then they were in the dressing room again and the lovely tutus were whisked away, back into their boxes.

Each time they went to change, the costumes got a bit simpler and the photo backgrounds changed to plain-coloured paper as they ended up doing ordinary leotards in different colours with and without little overskirts. Then Barry took a few close-up shots of ballet shoes and it was all over. When the time came, they weren't really sorry.

'I didn't know how tiring it would be,' said Emma wearily.

'It's worse if you're not used to it,' said Shell.

'You did a great job!' said her mum.

'It was good fun,' said Jem, 'and at

least I didn't have to wear embroidered jackets . . . I just hope none of the boys at school ever get to see the catalogue.'

'I'm planning to take it into school to show to all my friends!' Lou told him.

'Do it and you die!' said Jem darkly.

Chapter Six

Mrs Pinkham knew a restaurant by the riverside where they could get a quick meal before the show. Lou sat and watched the silvery sparkles as an evening breeze ruffled the water. She was feeling so happy that she couldn't remember *ever* feeling happier. It had been brilliant modelling all the ballet clothes and now, unbelievably, it seemed that she had also earned quite a lot of money. She decided to save most of it for her ballet lessons. It was true that her mum had a job now and money was a bit easier, but it would be great to be able to say, 'I'll pay for the classes *with my own money*.' She had never had money of her own before.

'What are you grinning at?' asked Jem. 'You look like a cat that's been at the cream.'

'I *feel* like a cat that's been at the cream,' said Lou with a deep sigh of contentment, 'all fat and full up to the ears . . .'

At that moment their food arrived, so no one said anything much for the next ten minutes. Then Shell said, 'You'll love *West Side Story*. I've seen it twice already.' Seeing their surprise, she added, 'Their dance arranger used to be in Mum's dance troupe, so she gets us free tickets.'

'That's how it will be for me when you lot are all famous,' said Emma hopefully. 'You'll send me free tickets so that I can come and see you. Shell can send me musical tickets and Lou can give me ballet ones.'

'What about Jem?' asked Shell.

Jem didn't answer.

'I expect Jem will do musicals too,' said Emma, but Jem just smiled and went on munching.

Shell wanted an answer. '*Are* you going to do musicals?' she asked him.

He shrugged. 'Who knows?' he said. 'I might not be good enough.' He went on eating.

'But you do *want* to do musicals?'

'Well, of course (*munch, munch*). Musicals are brilliant.'

'So is ballet!' said Lou.

'Yes . . . OK, ballet is brilliant too (*munch, munch*). I like both of them.'

Shell didn't give up easily. 'But which do you want to do when you grow up?' she asked.

Jem frowned. He didn't seem to want to answer and Lou wondered if Paul had been right.

'Paul says you wouldn't tell if you did want to be a ballet dancer,' she said, 'because the boys would tease you at school.'

'Who's Paul?' asked Shell.

Lou remembered with a start that she had promised not to mention Paul. She glanced at Emma and saw that she was already turning pink. Luckily Shell didn't seem to have noticed, so Lou said quickly, 'Oh, just some boy at our ballet school. He's going to White Lodge next year.'

'Oh, lucky thing!' said Shell. 'That must be really exciting!'

Lou was surprised. 'Would *you* like to go to White Lodge?' she asked. 'I thought you only wanted to do musicals.'

Shell shrugged. 'Well, I'm too short for ballet,' she said, 'so I'd never get in. I wouldn't mind being a famous ballerina if I was a bit taller . . .' For a moment she looked wistful, then she laughed her loud laugh. 'Lucky I can sing as well as dance,' she said. 'You need to be a good singer to star in musicals.'

'Jem can't sing for toffee,' said Lou. 'I know, because I had to stand in front of him once in assembly. He just growls.'

Jem looked miffed. 'I never said I *could* sing,' he pointed out. 'I only want to be a dancer.'

'But then you wouldn't get to be the star,' said Lou, 'not in a musical.'

'Well, Shell can be the star!' Jem said it as if he didn't mind, but Lou thought that he did.

'If you do ballet you don't have to sing,' she said eagerly, 'then you *could* be the star.'

'Oh, *really*?' said Jem. 'I thought you just wanted me standing around to hold you up. I always thought *you* were going to be the star, doing your arabesques in your white tutu!'

Lou hesitated. The truth was that this

was exactly how she had imagined it. She
had never thought about Jem being a star,
only herself. Now she found herself
saying, 'Rudolf Nureyev was a star, and
there are lots of ballets where men dance
the lead, like that one with the pirate
where they do all that leaping about!'

'Musicals are much more fun,' said
Shell. She seemed to feel that Lou was
getting the best of the argument.

Jem was beginning to look a bit hunted, so Mrs Pinkham said, 'Now, girls, stop giving the poor boy a hard time. He's got years yet before he needs to make up his mind between ballet and musicals. All he has to decide now is what he wants for his afters,' and she handed them the big glossy menu.

Chapter Seven

'I hope you'll be able to see all right,' said Mrs Pinkham anxiously as the taxi sped them on their way to the theatre. 'I had fixed us some nice seats at the front of the circle, but that was for the afternoon show. When we had to change them for the evening, I said we would take any seats they had left.' She seemed worried that her outing would be spoilt.

'But if Barry hadn't had his accident, we wouldn't have come to the shoot,' said

Jem comfortingly, 'so it doesn't matter if our seats aren't so good.'

'Oh no, we won't mind a bit,' said Lou. 'I mean, we wouldn't have missed the modelling for anything.'

Mrs Pinkham brightened up. 'Well, so long as you're not disappointed.'

But when they reached the theatre they found a surprise in store. Their tickets had been left at the box office for them and there was a note in the envelope from Mrs Pinkham's friend. Shell's mum read it and then she smiled at them all.

'Come on,' she said. 'I don't think you're going to be disappointed.' She led them through into the stalls, down the centre aisle and into the very front row.

'Oh, brilliant, Mum!' said Shell. 'But how on earth did you get seats like this at the very last minute?'

'Well,' said Mrs Pinkham, 'it seems they were being kept for some important overseas visitors who are arranging for the company to tour in their country. But their plane has been delayed and they won't be arriving now until tomorrow.'

Lou couldn't believe her luck as they settled into the comfy plush seats. She wondered if people would think they were really important to be sitting in the front row and wished she had worn her posh frock . . . But before she could get too carried away, the lights dimmed and the overture began.

They knew the music well from their video of the film version and Lou could picture the opening scene with the gang of teenage boys stalking like hunting animals through the streets of the crumbling city . . .

The curtain rose, swiftly and silently,
and there they were, motionless and
threatening against a background of
seedy buildings and rusting fire escapes
. . . only this time they were *real* and very
close to her.

Lou caught her breath as they sprang
into action. Another gang appeared and a

fight broke out. Lou could see that every movement was planned and skilfully danced, as it had been in the film. But there was all the difference in the world between watching a fight on a small television screen and having it take place between flesh-and-blood actors so close that you felt you could reach out and touch them. One of the Sharks sprang from the back of the stage on to one of the rival gang, the Jets, only to be seized by him and thrown through the air. He came hurtling towards them and Lou felt Emma cowering back into her seat as it seemed that he must surely land on top of them. He landed on the very edge of the stage, spun around and leapt back into the fight.

Never had Lou felt her heart race as it did during that opening scene. For the

first time she thought she really knew
what it would be like to dance on stage in
a musical. She could see the tiny beads of
sweat on the dancers' faces as they
jumped and somersaulted. And as if that
wasn't difficult enough, they had to sing
too! Lou was really glad that she had

decided to be a ballet dancer. At least in ballet, she thought, you don't have to have enough breath left to burst into song!

Chapter Eight

'The fight scene was best,' said Jem,
'especially that bit where the guy nearly
ended up in the audience!'

'Oh, he does that every night,' said
Shell, 'and he always lands right on the
edge of the stage. He knows just what
he's doing.'

They were sitting in the front row
eating ice-creams in the interval. Mrs
Pinkham had gone off somewhere.

'I liked the bit where Tony and Maria

were in the bridal shop,' said Lou with a sigh.

'Oh, the *romantic* bit,' said Jem. 'I bet you were having a little weep in the dark!'

Lou glared at him, but before she could hit back, Emma said, 'I liked that too, but my favourite was the "America" scene, because that's the one we did at the Summer School.'

'But it wasn't the same,' Lou pointed

out. 'I mean, *we* did it with boys against girls like in the film, but they did it with just the girls from the Sharks' gang.'

'Well, that's how it was written for the stage,' said Shell. 'The film people changed it because there's more room in a film studio. A theatre stage is really too small for them all at once.'

'That's what made the fight so brilliant,' said Jem, 'getting all that action into such a small space.'

The audience were coming back to their seats but Mrs Pinkham was nowhere to be seen. She arrived, rather breathless, just as the lights dimmed and Lou thought she looked very pleased about something.

The second half of the show was the sad part, as Tony and Maria's love affair was destroyed by the rivalry between the

two gangs. Lou and Emma knew what
was coming, but they still shed tears.
They were relieved to find that Shell's
mum had armed herself with a pack of
tissues, which she handed along the row.
When the cast took their curtain calls,
they clapped until their hands hurt. The
performers were so close, it seemed to
Lou that their smiles were meant for her
alone. As the red curtain fell between
them, she felt she had been suddenly
parted from friends.

'Well, you've had a heavy day,' said
Mrs Pinkham. 'Are you all worn out?'

'Oh no!' said Lou. 'I mean, I *was* tired
at the end of the shoot, but now I'm wide
awake again.'

The others agreed.

'Then maybe you'd like a quick trip
round to the stage door?'

'Oh yes, please!' said Emma. 'Then we could get our programmes signed.'

They hurried through the crowded foyer, out into the street and down a dark alley at the side of the theatre. Emma's face fell when she saw the crowd of fans already gathered at the stage door. But Mrs Pinkham led them straight on, saying, 'Excuse me' and 'May we come through, please?'

Emma looked nervous. She thought the other people might object, telling them to wait their turn. But when they reached the stage door, Shell's mum waved them inside.

They found themselves in a dull little room with green-painted brick walls. On one side was a glass window like a ticket office where the stage-door keeper kept guard. Mrs Pinkham seemed to know him well, and was just asking after his family when a blonde woman came hurrying through the door that led into the theatre.

'Hi, Jackie! Hi there, Shell!' she said, kissing them both. 'And these must be your friends.'

Shell introduced them all.

'I hear you're keen dancers,' she said as they shook hands. 'We'll need you in a few years' time.'

'Got to keep them coming,' said Mrs Pinkham, and the two women laughed.

Does she mean that *we'll* be the ones dancing on stage, wondered Lou, with fans waiting for *us* at the stage door? She had often dreamed of it but now, in a real theatre, it was hard to believe that it would ever happen . . . And yet Mrs Pinkham and her friend spoke as if it would be the most natural thing in the world.

'I thought you'd like a quick peep backstage,' said Shell's mum, 'but we won't hang around because it's late and you'll see a lot of the dancers at the barbecue tomorrow.'

'Oh, are they coming?' said Lou excitedly. She had lots of questions she wanted to ask about dancing in musicals.

'Well, they're all invited,' said Mrs Pinkham.

Her friend led them down dusty, bare passageways, and up and down little flights of steps. The backstage of the theatre was very different from the gold and red plush of the auditorium. Now and then she would knock and open a door, giving them a glimpse into the dressing rooms where the dancers sat

before rows of lighted mirrors, busily
removing their stage make-up.

'Give me your programmes,' said
Shell's mum's friend. 'I'll pass them
around and then bring them to the
barbecue tomorrow.'

When they reached the front of the
theatre again, Shell's dad was waiting.

They piled into the big car and tiredness hit them like a wall. They were all fast asleep long before they reached Shell's house.

Chapter Nine

Lou felt the sunlight on her face and turned over. She opened her eyes a crack but it was too bright, so she closed them again. She had been dreaming that she was in America but she couldn't quite remember the dream . . . only that there had been a lot of dancing.

So where am I really? she wondered. Her quick glimpse of the room had shown her white floaty curtains moving in the breeze from an open window . . .

And wasn't there a bed too, draped around with white hangings, or was that part of the dream?

Shading her eyes with one hand, she opened them again and looked around.

'Oh, wow!' she breathed.

The bed with the floaty curtains was a four-poster, the sort of bed Princess Aurora might have slept in in *The Sleeping Beauty*. But the head that lay sleeping on the embroidered pillows had bright-blue hair.

'Are you awake, Lou?'

It was Emma's voice and Lou turned to see her friend propped up on one elbow in a divan bed against the wall, not far from her own.

'Isn't Shell's room *amazing*?' said Emma softly.

'Like a film set,' agreed Lou, sitting up to get a better look.

The big sunlit room was all pink and white, with touches of gold. There were lots of shelves with dolls and china ornaments and things, and a whole heap

of cuddly stuffed animals on the floor.
Then Lou noticed that the window with
the white floaty curtains was really a
glass door leading out on to a balcony.
She jumped out of bed and went to
investigate. Emma followed close behind.

The balcony overlooked a large garden
with close-cut lawns and neat flowerbeds
full of bright flowers. Below them was a
terrace with a big blue swimming pool,
where Shell's dad, in bright flower-
patterned bathing trunks, was swimming
up and down. He was splashing a lot and
breathing heavily, rather like a friendly
porpoise.

'Good morning!' called Lou, and he
looked up.

'Morning, girls! Is my Shell up yet?'

'She's still asleep,' Lou told him.

'Typical!' he said. 'Never can wake up

in the mornings. Come and have a dip.'

The sound of voices had brought Jem
out on to another balcony. Mrs Pinkham
appeared on the terrace below.

'Come on down, loves,' she called up.
'I told your mums to pack your
swimming gear.'

Five minutes later the three friends
were in the pool, splashing and shouting.

'Shell is missing all the fun,' said Jem.
'You'd think the noise would have woken
her.'

Mrs Pinkham laughed. 'Not our Shell,'
she said. 'She's a real performer. Wide
awake until midnight and then sleeps
until lunchtime.'

'Doesn't she like to swim?' asked
Emma.

'Well, she won't swim this morning,'
said Mrs Pinkham. 'She'll want to keep

that blue hairdo intact for the barbecue!'

'I can hear you all talking about me,' said a small sleepy voice.

They looked up and saw Shell on her balcony, rubbing her eyes, which were half-closed against the light.

'Come and swim,' called Jem.

But Shell shuddered. 'Can't take all this sunshine,' she said, covering her eyes. Then she turned and went slowly back through the moving white curtains.

She's like someone in a film, thought Lou, as she watched her go. It was easy to believe that Shell would be a star one day, but she did make Lou feel so *very* ordinary.

Half an hour later they were sitting round a low table eating their breakfast. Shell sat with her back to the light and smiled sleepily.

'Your room is really lovely, Shell,' said Emma, looking around her.

Shell sighed. 'Do you like it?' she asked. 'My mum decorated it.'

'Don't *you* like it?' said Emma, surprised.

'Well, it's all right,' said Shell, 'but I'd like something wild and jazzy, with bright colours and things.'

'Why didn't you tell your mum what you wanted?' asked Lou.

Shell frowned and thought about it. 'Well,' she said at last, 'when Mum was my age, they were very poor, see . . . She had to share this tiny room with two of her sisters. She had a dream of having a room like this, with the bed and the white curtains and all that . . . And you know what mums are, they want to give *you* all the things *they* couldn't have . . . And then they're so thrilled, you can't tell them it's not what you wanted.'

'Like your mum at your party,' said Lou to Emma.

'Oh yes,' said Emma. 'All those balloons and decorations – like a little child's party! It was *so* embarrassing.'

'I bet when *you* grow up,' said Jem to Shell, 'you'll give your daughter a wild jazzy room.'

'Yes,' said Lou, 'and *she'll* be dreaming of a four-poster bed like Princess Aurora's!'

Shell laughed her loud laugh and set them all giggling. When they had calmed down again, Lou asked Shell, 'Will some of the dancers from last night *really* be coming to your barbecue?'

'Oh, quite a few, I should think,' said Shell casually. 'I mean, it's a good lunch, isn't it, and a dip in the pool. They often come round.'

'If we'd had the barbecue last night,' said Jem, 'the way your mum planned it, the dancers would all have been on stage.'

They thought about it and Emma asked, 'Will Barry be coming?'

'With free drinks?' said Shell. 'Nothing will keep him away!'

'Then we ought to be really nice to him,' said Emma, 'because if he hadn't fallen off his bike and hurt himself, we wouldn't have got to do the modelling and the dancers wouldn't be coming to the barbecue and *everything*.'

'Yeah,' said Shell, 'that's true, Em. Funny how things turn out.'

Chapter Ten

Barry sat with his leg propped up in a cushioned garden chair and thought, rather hazily, that it was one of the best barbecues he could remember. For some reason he didn't quite understand, he was being waited on hand and foot.

'Are you sure you've got everything you need?' asked Emma. 'Only Lou and me, we wanted to go and see some of the dancers.'

Barry surveyed the table beside him:

plates piled with steak and chicken, a big bowl of salad, a large basket full of bread rolls and a whole stack of beer cans.

'I reckon I could survive for about half an hour,' he told them solemnly.

'Right!' said Emma, looking at her watch. 'We'll be back about twenty-past then.'

'Great,' said Barry, reaching for a can and sticking his finger into the ring-pull. He watched the two girls as they hurried away and shook his head. Kids are really weird sometimes, he thought.

The dancers were mostly in the pool, all looking incredibly sleek and glamorous. Shell was sitting near the edge, chatting to them. She was wearing a blue and green patterned swimsuit to match her hair and a sarong skirt. Jem sat beside her, soaking up the atmosphere.

'Why does Shell always look more like one of them than one of us?' sighed Lou enviously. 'I mean, as if she was a professional already.'

'Well, she is, sort of,' said Emma, 'with all that modelling . . .'

'I suppose so,' said Lou.

'Would you like to be her?' asked Emma. 'I mean, she can't get much time to just hang about with her friends.'

'That's true,' said Lou. She thought about it and then added, 'She never talks about her friends . . . not friends our age.'

'Do you think she even has a "best friend"?' asked Emma. 'I mean, if she had, you'd think she would have invited her today so we could meet her.'

Lou watched Shell talking and joking, very much at ease with the older dancers. Then she turned to Emma. 'I think I'd really rather be us,' she decided.

Emma smiled. 'So would I,' she said.

'I wouldn't mind doing a bit more modelling though,' said Lou. 'Do you think our mums will let us?'

'They'll be here soon,' said Emma. 'We can ask them.'

They had got their programmes back and the dancers had all signed next to their photographs inside. There were programme notes too, about where they had done their dance training. Some of them had been to dance schools Lou had never even heard of. They were beginning to come out of the pool now in search of food and drink.

'Let's go and thank them for signing our programmes,' suggested Lou. 'Then we can say we've actually *spoken* to them.'

This took quite a while. Some of them just said, 'You're welcome!' but others stopped to chat and to answer their questions about dancing. Somewhere along the way they joined up with Jem and Shell again.

Then Emma's mum and dad arrived, bringing Lou's mum and Charlie with them. Jem's grandparents came close behind.

Mrs Pinkham was a big fan of Orly Sinclair, who was a jazz singer. She came over all dithery when they were introduced. Lou could hear her laughing nervously as she told Orly that she had *every one* of her records. Jem seemed quite used to seeing his grandmother get this sort of attention. But as Lou hugged Jenny and Charlie she felt pleased that her mum was just *her mum* and that she didn't have to share her with anyone else.

Suddenly Emma glanced at her watch. 'Oh no!' she said. 'It's quarter-to and we forgot all about Barry! We were taking

care of him,' she explained to Shell,
'because of his poor leg.'

'Oh, is *that* how he got hold of all that
beer!' said Shell. 'Well, you needn't
worry about him. He's dead to the
world!'

They looked across and saw that she
was right. Barry was stretched out in his
chair, snoring peacefully.

'Will he be all right?' asked Emma,
feeling a bit guilty.

'He'll be fine,' said Shell. 'Dad will
drive him home or else he'll stay over.
Mum's used to Barry. She's known him
ever since they lived next door to each
other in the East End . . . when they were
both kids.'

We'll be a bit like that, thought Lou.
When we're rich and famous, Shell will
give fantastic parties (it was easier to

imagine Shell as the hostess) and Emma
and I will be there, and Shell will say,
'This is Emma Browne and this is Lucy
Lambert, the famous ballerina. We've
been friends since we met at Summer
School when we were all kids . . .' She
smiled at the picture she had conjured up,
and then she remembered Jem. He would
be at the parties too, but whose partner
would he be? Well, he can't sing, she
thought, that's for sure, and that just
might make all the difference . . .

As they drove home in the Brownes' car,
Lou and Emma told their parents all
about the shoot.

'Can we do it again?' asked Lou. 'I
mean, Shell makes heaps of money doing
modelling.'

'I think you've got quite enough to do,'

said Jenny, 'what with your school work and your dancing.'

'But it was just one afternoon,' pleaded Lou, 'and now I can help pay for my ballet lessons and things.'

'It will be a help,' agreed her mother. 'Perhaps next year you might get a chance to do that dance catalogue again.'

Lou sighed. 'Next year' seemed a long way away, but it was better than nothing.

'Tell us about *West Side Story*,' said Mrs Browne, changing the subject.

So Lou and Emma told them all about the seats in the front row and the dancer who looked as if he might land on top of them.

'I think we must go and see that, Val,' said Emma's dad. 'But I think we'll sit somewhere safe, like the upper circle!'

'Oh, Dad!' said Emma. 'He always

stops just on the edge of the stage. Shell said so and she's seen it three times!'

'Better safe than sorry,' said Mr Browne.

There was a comfortable silence as they drove along and then Lou said, 'It was the best weekend *ever*.'

'You're always saying things are the *best ever*,' said Jenny. 'Your life must be getting better and better all the time.'

Lou thought about it. 'Yes,' she said. 'I reckon it is. Ever since we took up dancing, it just gets more and more exciting. Doesn't it, Em?'

And Emma agreed that it did.

DANCING SHOES

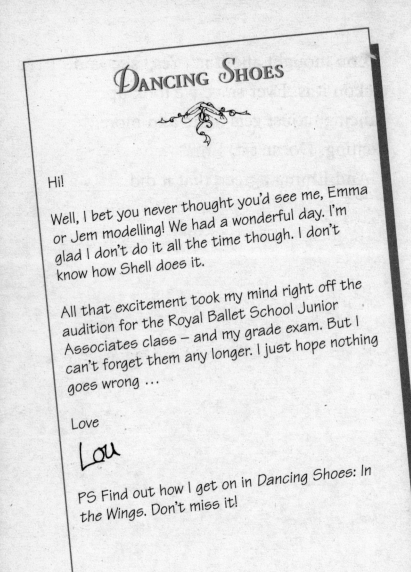

Hi!

Well, I bet you never thought you'd see me, Emma or Jem modelling! We had a wonderful day. I'm glad I don't do it all the time though. I don't know how Shell does it.

All that excitement took my mind right off the audition for the Royal Ballet School Junior Associates class – and my grade exam. But I can't forget them any longer. I just hope nothing goes wrong …

Love

Lou

PS Find out how I get on in Dancing Shoes: In the Wings. Don't miss it!